BIG HORSE LITTLE HORSE

BIG HORSE LITTLE HORSE

By Martha Goldberg

drawn by Tom Funk

The Macmillan Company
New York

Library of Congress catalog card number: 60–14296

First Printing

The Macmillan Company, New York
Brett-Macmillan Ltd., Galt, Ontario

Printed in the United States of America

for Ethel

One morning, just as the sun came up, Mateo brought his burro loaded with firewood down from the mountain. The little burro, almost buried under the heavy load, stopped to rest on the steep, rocky trail.

"Get up, slow one," Mateo said, tapping him lightly with a stick. "Mama is waiting for the wood."

Far below were the red tile roofs of the village that was Mateo's home. There each family made the black pottery which was famous over all of Mexico.

Today Mateo's mother, one of the finest potters of the village, would fire the ollas—the large water jars. So Mateo hurried with the wood.

For still another reason he hurried. He wanted to see the beautiful brown horse, Panchita, who belonged to Big Pablo.

On his way from the mountain he had often stopped to watch her. Then he had gone home and tried to model a clay horse. His horses had never looked like Panchita. Before he made another, Mateo wanted to see her again.

Mateo was sure that he could make a good clay horse. This was a secret that no one knew, not even his sister, Concha. Some-

day, he told himself, he would become a fine potter like his mother.

At the edge of the village the trail widened to a rough, dusty road. Then Mateo went more quickly. Near Big Pablo's home Panchita was out in the field. She raced in wide, joyful circles, her forelegs stretched forward, her neck arched and her tail held high. She rolled over, rubbing her back on the rough ground, her heels kicking the air like a colt. Mateo laughed to see her.

He saw now why his little clay horse had not looked like Panchita. He had given it long ears like a burrito! Panchita's ears were small. Her mane and tail were long and silky. "When I reach home," Mateo thought, "I will know how to make a clay horse that looks like her."

Big Pablo came toward him as he stood watching Panchita.

"Good day, senor," Mateo called out.

"Good day, Mateo," Big Pablo answered, stopping beside him. "Look well at Panchita, for soon she will be gone. I will take her to the Saturday Market."

Mateo was shocked. "You will sell Panchita!" he exclaimed. "What a pity."

How could anyone who owned so fine a horse want to sell her? "Panchita is worth many burritos," he said to Big Pablo. "She is big and strong and she runs very fast."

"That is true," Big Pablo answered, "but also Panchita eats much. I must sell her. May the Almighty One grant her a good home."

Mateo turned away too sad to speak. He drove the burro slowly between the rows of tall cactus that grew beside the road. If Panchita left the village he would never see her again. She must not leave! His family could

use a horse. He would ask his father to buy her.

When Mateo reached home his father called out, "Mama is waiting for the wood. Where have you been so long?"

"I stopped at Big Pablo's," Mateo answered.

"You stopped while we waited for you?" his father asked.

"Si," Mateo said, all in a rush, "Big Pablo is selling Panchita. Please, Papa, can we not buy her?"

"Do you know why Big Pablo sells her, little son?" his father asked.

"Si, Papa," Mateo said.

"Are we so rich, then, that I should buy a horse because my son has set his heart on it? A horse, ha! Next he will be asking that I buy a motorcar. Go unload the wood, foolish one. Let me hear no more about Panchita."

Without a word Mateo led the burro to the woodpile. Quickly he unloaded the little animal and stacked the wood. Then he took the burro to his father who was going back to the mountain for another load.

After his father left, Mateo went into the house for a lump of the greyish-brown clay. He returned to the woodpile and sat down on the ground behind it, with his back against the adobe wall of the house. He was hidden from the patio.

He began to work quickly with the clay. He rolled it into a ball, then wet his fingers in a bowl of muddy water and smoothed it. He pinched one end to form the head and the tiny ears. Then he made the legs and tail of small rolls of clay.

He held up the little horse to look at it. It was not right. A horse was harder to make than a clay whistle in the shape of a bird, or an angel whose wide skirt was a bell. These things his mother had taught him to make. But he knew he could make his horse now if there were time before someone discovered his hiding place.

He bent the soft clay legs. Now the little horse began to look like Panchita racing across the field. As he worked he thought of the answers he might have given his father. A horse would make quick work of plowing the cornfield. A horse could carry the pottery to market in large bags slung over her sides. He and Concha and Baby Rosita could all ride on her, too. Could a burro carry so much?

He could not tell his father these things, for one answer he did not have. What would they feed Panchita?

"Mateo! Mateo!" It was sister Concha calling him.

Mateo crouched lower against the house.

Concha soon tired of looking for him, for her voice faded away. All was quiet as Mateo worked. He scratched with his fingernail to make the mane. He used a tiny stick to mark the eyes and nose. Then with wet fingers he smoothed over the little body again.

"Mateo! You are there! Come here!"

It was Mama calling him this time. She sounded angry.

Mateo knew he must answer her. He stood up and squeezed through the narrow space between the woodpile and the house. Covering the clay horse with his hand he walked into the patio.

"I am here, Mamacita," he said.

"Why did you not come when I sent Conchita for you?" his mother asked.

Mateo held out the horse for her to see. "This I was making," he said. "I wished to finish it."

Mama took the little horse gently into her hands.

"It is good," she said, in a surprised voice.

"Then I may fire it?" Mateo asked eagerly.

"If you wish," Mama said, "but it is small and thin. I fear it will break in the firing."

"Then I shall make a larger one," Mateo said quickly.

"No, my son," his mother said shaking her head. "You must make the toys that we can sell. No one buys clay horses."

Mateo turned his head away to hide the tears in his eyes. Not to make a little horse like Panchita! Soon she would be gone forever! It was almost too much to bear.

His mother did not seem to notice how he felt. She went on talking. "Mateo, the little grandmother has a fever. I must take food to her. There is work for you to do while I am gone."

"Do you wish me to watch the fire?"

"I could not fire the water jars this morning," his mother said. "You came too late with the wood."

"For a little moment I watched Panchita," Mateo explained.

"Always you watch Panchita," his mother answered, sharply. "Will you never learn to come when we are waiting for you?"

Matco hung his head and said in a low voice, "It gives me great shame, Mama."

"Let it not repeat itself, little son," his mother said, shaking her finger at him. She went quickly to the house and brought out a large basket which she placed upon a table against the patio wall.

Then, seeing Mateo's sad face, she put her hand on his shoulder and said with a smile, "Today it is well that there is no fire to watch, since I must go away."

"I will go with you to the house of the little grandmother," Mateo offered.

"No, son," his mother said, "Rafael is bringing the tourists to see how the black pottery is made. You and Concha must be ready and place yourselves at their service."

Mama and Papa had good reason to be angry with him this morning, Mateo thought. If he showed them that he could do his work well, Mama might allow him to make a clay horse another day.

"Concha and I will do as you wish, Mamacita," he said. "When will you return?"

"In the bus that follows," his mother said. She moved about quickly as she spoke, in and out of the house and across the patio.

Mateo went after her, watching as she took tortillas, beans and chicken for grandmother and placed them in the basket. She covered the food with a clean, embroidered cloth.

Then she said, "You must sweep the patio and set out the chairs. Also have ready the clay. Cover it well with a wet cloth."

Mateo nodded.

"Put out a large olla, one that is almost dry. I will decorate it as the tourists watch," his mother added. "And place on the big table the toys and bowls we have made to sell."

"Si," Mateo said, "Concha and I will polish them well."

"Take care that you do all that I have told you," his mother said.

"Let it not worry you, Mamacita," Mateo answered.

Concha, who had been watching in the plaza, burst into the yard at that moment,

calling, "Mamacita! Mamacita! The bus! It comes."

"I will go now," Mama said.

She tied Baby Rosita tightly in her shawl. Then she placed a roll of cloth like a crown on the top of her head. On this she set the basket of food.

"Adios! Till we meet again," she said as she started down the road.

"Adios! Mamacita," Mateo and Concha answered. "Go with God."

Turning around Mama called back, "Mateo, look to the sky. Should it rain you must carry in the firewood and the jars that are drying in the sun."

"I will remember," Mateo called after her.

He could hear the loud horn of the bus that was waiting in the plaza to pick up passengers. A short while later as the bus started the horn blew again.

Concha took a corn husk broom and began to sweep the patio. Carrying a large olla of water, Mateo went after her, wetting the ground to settle the dust.

Next he and Concha carried the chairs into the patio. They put them in a half-circle, each with a view of the mat where Mama would sit to work the clay.

They cleaned off the big table and brought out the basket of small toys. These they polished with a soft cloth until the whistles and bells and little dishes of black pottery shone in the bright sunshine.

Mama would be pleased.

"Conchita," Mateo said, "go to the plaza and wait for the bus. Carry the little Rosita so that Mama may come quickly."

After Concha had gone, Mateo squatted on the ground. How his fingers wanted to make another clay horse, one that would remind him of Panchita. If only Mama had not forbidden it.

As he waited a few drops of rain fell. Then swiftly the clouds opened wide. The rain poured down in a solid wall of water.

Mateo jumped up. He must carry in the firewood. It should be dry when Mama made a fire in the kiln. The ollas he would get later.

He hurried to the woodpile and gathered an armload of branches. They tickled and scratched as he ran with them pressed against his body. Dropping them on the dry ground under the roof of the open shed, he ran back for more.

He came to the opening in the cactus fence and went quickly out to the road.

"Conchita! Conchita!" he called. He did not wait to see if she would come.

Running back to the woodpile he filled his arms again. His clothes dripped water and his bare feet were covered with mud. Back and forth he ran.

The rain poured down making puddles in the yard. Mateo saw that the clay ollas were standing in water. Should he stop and put them away before they were spoiled? But what good were clay jars without dry firewood?

"Conchita! Conchita!" he shouted again in his loudest voice. Even as he called, he was afraid she would not hear him above the noise of the rain.

One armload of wood was left. As Mateo turned to get it Concha came running in from the road.

Breathless, she picked up two of the large jars. She turned each one over and shook the water from it. She ran with the jars to the house setting them down on the dirt floor.

Mateo went to help her. She was ahead. He picked up two jars and, racing after her, called, "Who will arrive there first?"

He did not see the little pig scurrying across the yard until it was too late. Tripping over it, he fell. The pig ran away squealing. Mateo was left on the ground with broken pottery around him.

Concha stood over him laughing. Mateo got up and brushed the mud and bits of broken pottery from his hands and clothes. His face was very solemn. Again he had done something wrong!

"They were fine, big ollas," he said shaking his head sadly. "I cannot make others for Mama. She will be angry with me."

"But I will tell my mother that the little pig threw himself before you," Concha assured him.

Carrying the big jars two at a time, they put them all on the floor of the house. When they had finished they stood in the open doorway and watched the rain. After a few moments, Mateo went out into the yard again to see if they had forgotten anything. Every stick of firewood and all the drying clay were under cover. He let out his breath in relief.

Walking back to Concha he said, "You came from the plaza just in time."

The plaza! The bus! In his hurry Mateo had forgotten it.

"Did not the bus arrive?" he asked.

Concha shook her head. "They say it sits by the bridge over the river and cannot go."

"Soon the tourists will come," Mateo said, "and my mother is not here."

"Mamacita will come on foot," Concha said.

"Si," Mateo answered, "but the tourists in the cars will come before."

While they talked, the rain stopped just

as suddenly as it had begun. The sun shone again in a bright blue sky. The chairs were drying. The water in the puddles was soaking into the ground.

There was the sound of cars in the road. Car doors slammed. People were talking. Rafael, the guide, followed by the tourists, walked into the patio.

Mateo ran to Rafael and drew him aside. "All is ready," he whispered, "but Mama is not here. She went this morning to the house of my grandmother, and the bus does not come back with her."

"Do not worry yourself," Rafael said. "I shall show the kiln and the clay, also the clay things your mother has made. She will come before long."

Mateo felt better then. He turned to Concha and said, "Go again to the plaza and wait for Mama."

Concha left the patio quickly.

Mateo stood near the table where the tourists were looking at the small toys. He did not understand their words, but he could tell that they admired the fine work. He was proud. These toys he and Concha had made. If the little clay horse were here on the table, Mateo wondered, would they like it, too?

Rafael now called everyone together in the patio. He told how Papa had dug the clay from the bank of the river and cleaned out all the coarse sand and rocks. He told how Mama and Papa wet the dry clay and worked it with their hands until it was soft and ready to use.

Rafael took the tourists into the house and showed them the water jars that Mateo and Concha had set upon the floor. He pointed out the other clay pieces and explained their uses, cooking pots, baking dishes and bowls for eating.

"Now," Rafael said, "we will go into the yard to see the kiln where the pottery is fired. Only the potters of this village know the secret of making it black."

To make the kiln, Papa had dug a deep hole in the ground. Near the bottom he had made a shelf of bricks. Rafael showed how Mama stacked the clay pieces on the shelf and how she covered them with bits of broken pottery. He showed the place underneath the brick shelf where Mama built the fire. He told how she closed both the kiln and the fire with earth, so that the pottery would bake properly.

Now the time had come when Mama would sit on the straw mat to make an olla. She would start with a ball of clay and whirl it round and round on two plates, one set on the bottom of the other. After she had pounded and patted the clay into a large jar she would set it aside to dry. Then she would decorate an olla that had already dried.

This was the most important part of the

visit and Mama was not here. The tourists had gone back into the patio and were seating themselves in the chairs. What should he and Rafael do, Mateo wondered?

He ran to the cactus fence and looked down the road. Beyond the cars the muddy road stretched empty to the plaza. There he saw people still waiting for the bus that sat by the river and would not move.

If Papa were here, he would take Mama's place on the mat and make an olla. But it was many hours before Papa would return. Mama had asked him, Mateo, to serve the tourists. He must do what he could.

Mateo walked back into the patio and said to Rafael in a low voice, "I can decorate an olla. Perhaps, in the meantime, Mama will come."

"With pleasure, Mateo," Rafael said. "It is well that you have thought about it."

Rafael spoke to the people seated in the chairs. "Today, Mateo will decorate an olla. He is only eight years old but already he is a good potter."

Mateo had brought from the house a large olla. It had been drying for several days but had not been fired. With a sharp, thin bit of stone, as he had seen his mother do, he made fine lines in a pattern around the neck

of the olla. Then on the widest part he drew a large flower with stem and leaves.

For a moment he held the olla up to show what he had done. Then he turned the stone over and used the smooth, flat side to polish the jar. He stopped and again held it up. With the flower on its polished side it was beautiful. He set it aside, for it was ready to fire.

Mateo had worked as long as he could, hoping that meanwhile Mama would come. Now he was finished and she was not here.

Some of the tourists were standing up and moving about the patio. Soon they would go away. They would not have seen, as Rafael had promised them, how the black pottery was made.

If only Mama would come, Mateo thought.

He stood up and ran quickly out to the road again. Down near the plaza someone was walking. Even so far away Mateo could see that it was not Mama. It was a man with a horse, Big Pablo leading Panchita away from the village!

A tear slid down Mateo's cheek. "Adios Panchita," he said softly. "Go with God."

Everything had gone wrong this day, he thought, as he turned and walked slowly back toward the patio. Now Panchita was on her way to market, and the tourists were leaving. He had not been able to show them, as Mama would have done, how to make the black pottery.

He reached the patio and found the tourists still there. If only he could make an olla, but Mama had said that he was too small to work with the large jars. If he made a little toy whistle or a bell no one would be able to see.

He could make a horse like the beautiful Panchita! Today Mama had said that his

little horse was good. Should he make a larger one while the people watched?

He had already done so many things wrong, and Mama had told him not to make a larger horse. But it was the only thing he

could do. When Mama came he would explain. Only sometimes she did not listen, he thought sadly, but punished swiftly.

Mateo sat down on the mat and picked up a lump of the wet clay. Quickly he shaped the round body, small head and tiny ears.

The people began to watch him work. Those who had been standing sat down.

He made the arched neck with the mane flying in the wind. With rolls of clay he formed the legs. Another roll made the tail which he flattened with a wet finger. How like Panchita the little horse was beginning to look!

Smiling with pleasure, Mateo held up his work. The people watching smiled back. Looking beyond them, Mateo saw his mother. She stood behind the row of chairs with Rafael and Concha. She had been watching as he worked with the clay!

Mateo felt his fingers grow stiff. The little horse was again a lump of cold, wet clay in his hands. He wanted to drop it and run away. His mother was a fine potter. Some said she was the finest in all of Mexico. He could not work as she watched. It was she who should be here on the mat.

Putting the horse down, Mateo motioned to his mother to come and take his place. She shook her head. Thinking that she did not understand, he stood up and walked toward her. Again she shook her head, then pointed to the mat.

Mateo went back to it and sat down. Slowly he picked up the little horse. Mama wanted him to finish! He could hardly believe that it was so. But she was smiling and waiting for him to go on.

He took up a sharp stick and drew the eyes. His fingernail made the fine lines on

the mane and tail to look like hair. Wetting his fingers in the bowl of water, he smoothed over the little body. He was finished.

He looked up at his mother.

She came forward, and Mateo said quickly, "I could not make an olla like yours, Mamacita. I made the big horse like Panchita because I could make nothing else."

"You did well, Mateo," his mother answered. She took the clay horse from him and turned it over carefully. "It is well made, little son," she said. "It will fire well."

Those were the finest words Mama could say. A rush of happiness flooded over Mateo.

The people had left their chairs and were crowding round and talking to Rafael.

"Many would like to buy the horse when it is fired," Rafael said to Mateo. "Will you make others?"

"I do not know," Mateo said, his eyes questioning his mother.

She smiled at him and nodded.

"Si," Mateo said proudly, "I will make many more."

Yes, he thought, he would make more horses like the lovely Panchita, and always

he would remember her. But he would learn to make other things of the black pottery, beautiful things that had never been made before. He would become one of the fine potters of the village.